GW00507882

Guest Spot

CLASSIC BLUES
Playalong *for* Flute

This publication is not authorised for sale in the
United States of America and/or Canada

WISE PUBLICATIONS
London/New York/Paris/Sydney/Copenhagen/Madrid

Exclusive Distributors:
Music Sales Limited
8/9 Frith Street, London W1V 5TZ, England.
Music Sales Pty Limited
120 Rothschild Avenue, Rosebery, NSW 2018, Australia.

Order No. AM941754
ISBN 0-7119-6267-7
This book © Copyright 1998 by Wise Publications.

Unauthorised reproduction of any part of this publication by
any means including photocopying is an infringement of copyright.

Book design by Michael Bell Design.
Compiled by Peter Evans.
Music arranged by Jack Long & Paul Honey.
Music processed by Enigma Music Production Services.
Cover photography by George Taylor.

Printed in the United Kingdom by
Page Bros. Limited, Norwich, Norfolk.

CD recorded by Passionhouse Music.
Instrumental solos by John Whelan.
Produced by Paul Honey.

Your Guarantee of Quality:
As publishers, we strive to produce every book to
the highest commercial standards.
The music has been freshly engraved and the book has been
carefully designed to minimise awkward page turns and
to make playing from it a real pleasure.
Particular care has been given to specifying acid-free, neutral-sized
paper made from pulps which have not been elemental chlorine bleached.
This pulp is from farmed sustainable forests and was
produced with special regard for the environment.
Throughout, the printing and binding have been planned to
ensure a sturdy, attractive publication which should give years of enjoyment.
If your copy fails to meet our high standards,
please inform us and we will gladly replace it.

Music Sales' complete catalogue describes thousands of
titles and is available in full colour sections by subject,
direct from Music Sales Limited.
Please state your areas of interest and send a
cheque/postal order for £1.50 for postage to:
Music Sales Limited, Newmarket Road, Bury St. Edmunds, Suffolk IP33 3YB.

Guest Spot

Fingering Guide

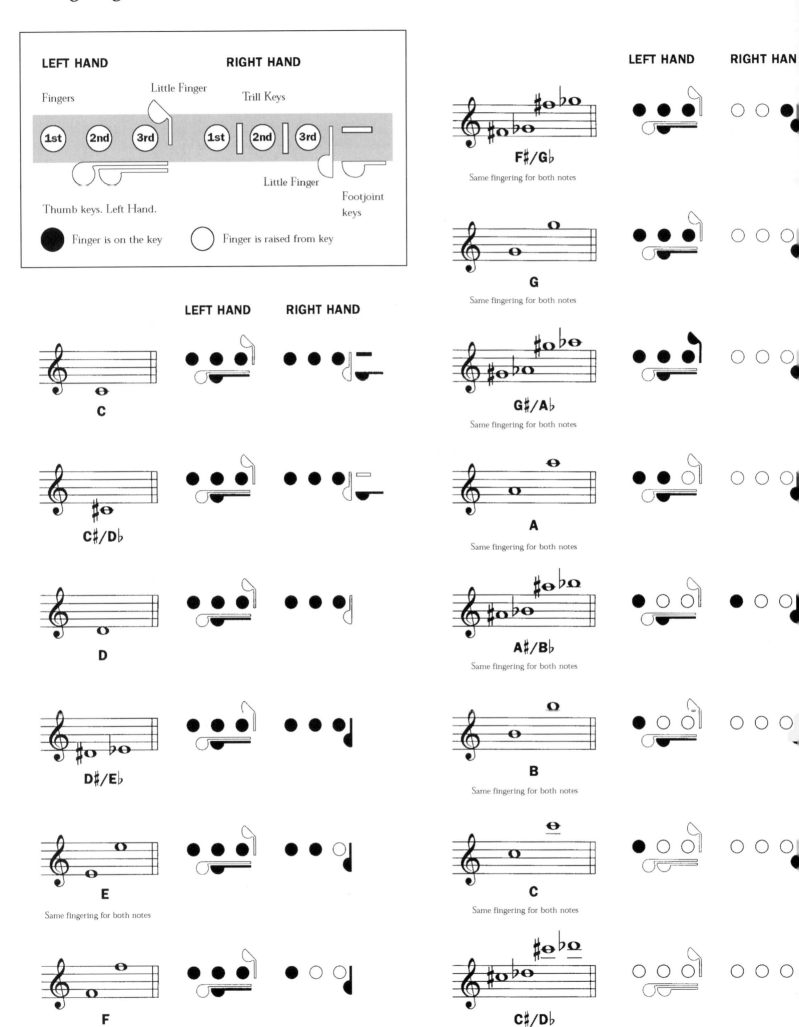

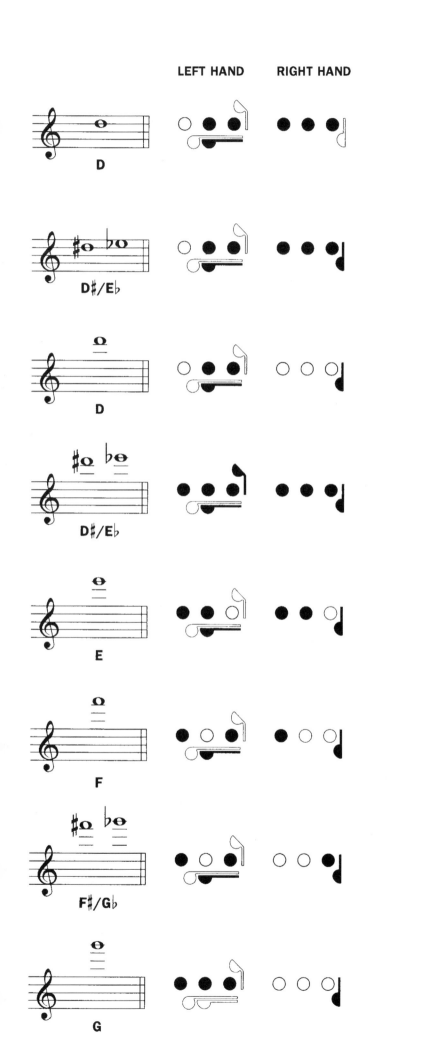

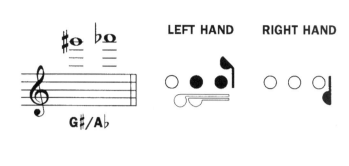

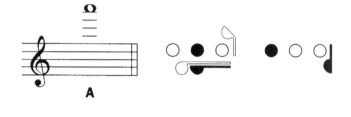

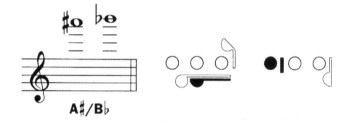

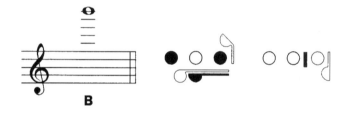

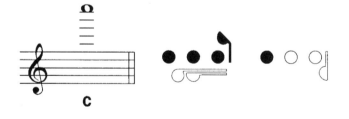

Cry Me A River

Words & Music by Arthur Hamilton

Double tempo

© Copyright 1955 Chappell & Company Incorporated, USA.
Warner Chappell Music Limited, 129 Park Street, London W1.
All Rights Reserved. International Copyright Secured.

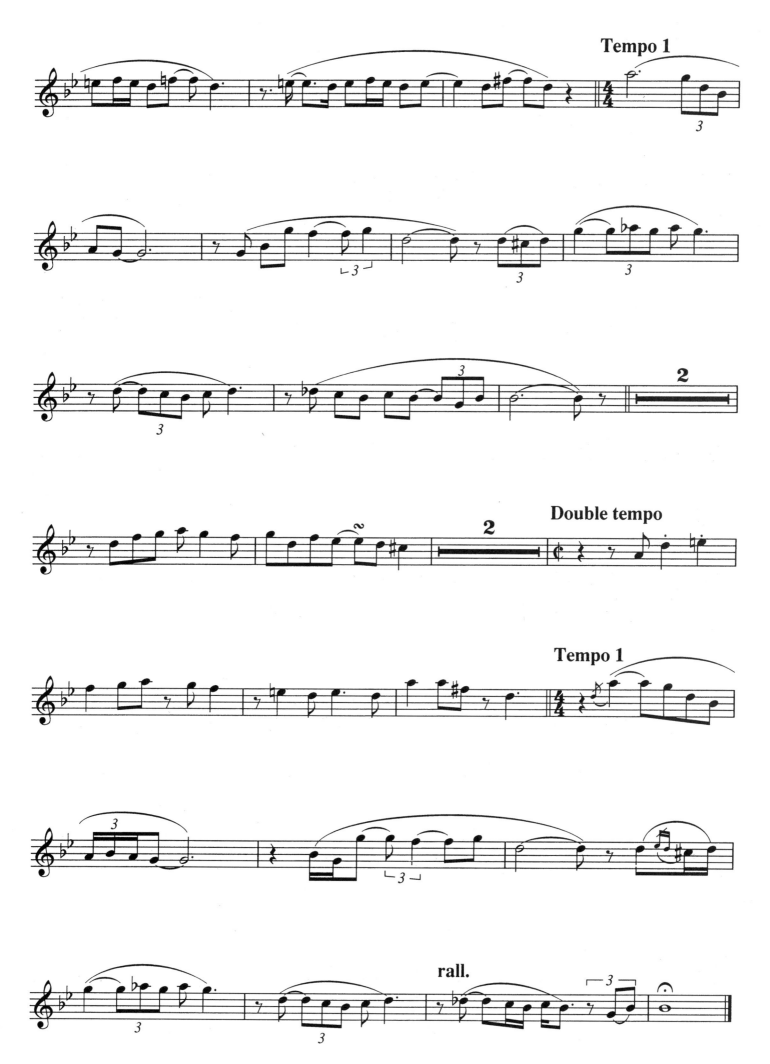

Fever

Words & Music by John Davenport & Eddie Cooley

Medium tempo (♩ = 120)

To Coda ⊕

© Copyright 1956 Jay and Cee Music Corporation assigned to Fort Knox Music Company, USA.
Lark Music Limited, Iron Bridge House, 3 Bridge Approach, London NW1 for the United Kingdom,
British Commonwealth (excluding Canada and Australasia), the Republic of Ireland and Israel.
All Rights Reserved. International Copyright Secured.

CODA

God Bless' The Child

Words & Music by Arthur Herzog Jr. & Billie Holiday

© Copyright 1941 Edward B. Marks Music Company, USA.
Carlin Music Corporation, Iron Bridge House, 3 Bridge Approach, London NW1.
All Rights Reserved. International Copyright Secured.

Li'l Darlin'

By Neal Hefti

Medium slow (♩ = 80)

To ⊕ Coda

© Copyright 1958 Neal Hefti Music Incorporated, USA.
Cinephonic Music Limited, 8/9 Frith Street, London W1.
All Rights Reserved. International Copyright Secured.

D.S. al Coda

CODA

Harlem Nocturne

Music by Earle Hagen
Words by Dick Rogers

© Copyright 1940, 1946 & 1951 Shapiro Bernstein & Company Incorporated, USA.
Peter Maurice Music Company Limited, 127 Charing Cross Road, London WC2.
All Rights Reserved. International Copyright Secured.

Hit The Road Jack

Words & Music by Percy Mayfield

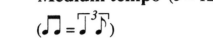

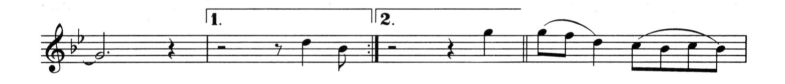

© Copyright 1961 Tangerine Music Corporation, USA.
Controlled in the UK & Eire by Rondor Music (London) Limited, 10a Parsons Green, London SW6.
All Rights Reserved. International Copyright Secured.

I Wish I Knew How It Would Feel To Be Free

By Billy Taylor

Medium tempo (♩ = 102)

© Copyright 1964, 1968 Duane Music Incorporated, USA.
Westminster Music Limited, Suite 2.07, Plaza 535 Kings Road, London SW10.
All Rights Reserved. International Copyright Secured.

D. 𝄋 *al Coda*

⊕ **CODA**

Moonglow

Words & Music by Will Hudson, Eddie de Lange & Irving Mills

Medium swing (♩ = 120)

© Copyright 1934 Exclusive Publications Incorporated, USA. Copyright assigned 1934 to Mills Music Incorporated, USA.
Authorised for sale in the UK and Eire only by permission of Boosey & Hawkes Music Publishers Limited, London.
All Rights Reserved. International Copyright Secured.

Swingin' Shepherd Blues

Words by Rhoda Roberts & Kenny Jacobson
Music by Moe Koffman

© Copyright 1957 Benell Music Company, USA. Now Adam R. Levy & Father Enterprises Incorporated, USA.
Sub-published by EMI Music Publishing Limited, 127 Charing Cross Road, London WC2.
All Rights Reserved. International Copyright Secured.

D.$ al Coda

CODA

Round Midnight

By Cootie Williams & Thelonious Monk

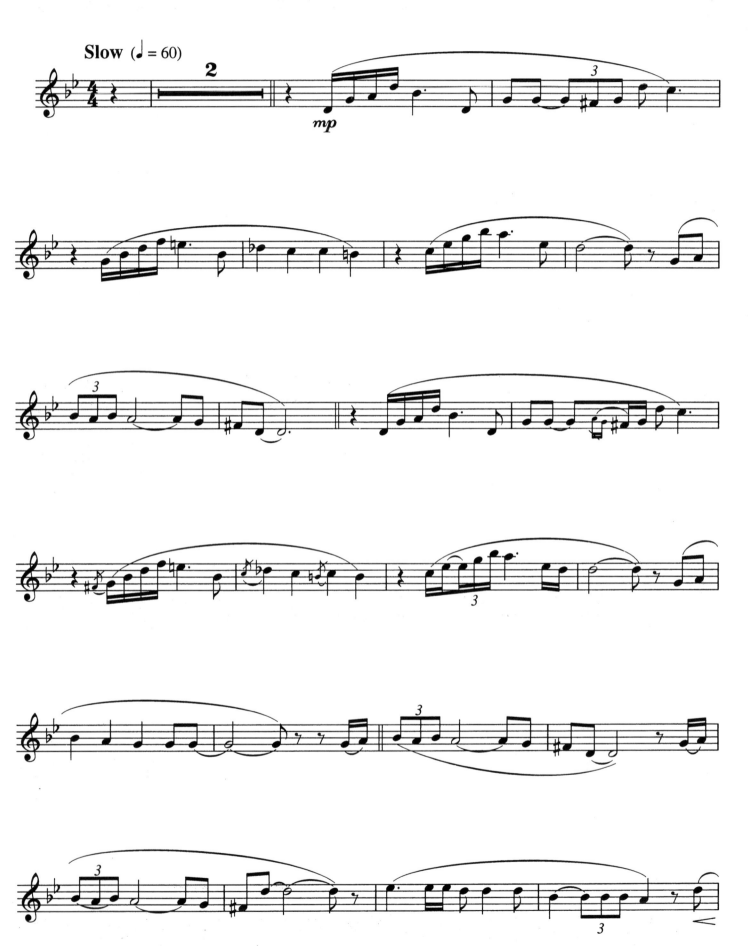

© Copyright 1944 by Advanced Music Corporation, USA.
Warner Chappell Music Limited, 129 Park Street, London W1.
All Rights Reserved. International Copyright Secured.

1/06 (57530)

Track Listing

Full instrumental performances...

1. **Cry Me A River**
   (Hamilton) Warner Chappell Music Limited.

2. **Fever**
   (Davenport/Cooley) Lark Music Limited.

3. **God Bless' The Child**
   ((Herzog Jr./Holiday) Carlin Music Corporation.

4. **Li'l Darlin'**
   (Hefti) Cinephonic Music Limited.

5. **Harlem Nocturne**
   (Hagen/Rogers) Peter Maurice Music Company Limited.

6. **Hit The Road Jack**
   (Mayfield) Rondor Music (London) Limited.

7. **I Wish I Knew How It Would Feel To Be Free**
   (Taylor) Westminster Music Limited.

8. **Moonglow**
   (Hudson/de Lange/Mills) Boosey & Hawkes Music Publishers Limited.

9. **Swingin' Shepherd Blues**
   (Roberts/Jacobson/Koffman) EMI Music Publishing Limited.

10. **Round Midnight**
    (Williams/Monk) Warner Chappell Music Limited.

Backing tracks only...

11. **Cry Me A River**

12. **Fever**

13. **God Bless' The Child**

14. **Li'l Darlin'**

15. **Harlem Nocturne**

16. **Hit The Road Jack**

17. **I Wish I Knew How It Would Feel To Be Free**

18. **Moonglow**

19. **Swingin' Shepherd Blues**

20. **Round Midnight**

MCPS

All rights of the record producer and the owners of the works reproduced reserved. Copying, public performances and broadcasting of this recording is prohibited.